Well?

"Thanks" for listening. We gotta do this again sometime.

Yeah, thought so.

...she seems awfully lonely recently.

She never gets to hang with us 'cuz of her job.

Fine by me!

Oh, I'm sure she's all right.

* SERENITY: BAD GIRL IN TOWN -- ed.

You seem pretty quiet tonight.

He noticed me !!!

Yeah, well, I didn't have anything to say.

Last race, Derek ! I want you as my partner !

Ready to go ?

...I was born ready...

Wanna come in, get sumthin' to eat?

Well... it's kinda late... your mom...

Don't worry 'bout her.

Try this. I **think** it's guacamole.

So how come you fall for all this Christian stuff?

* Methamphetamine

'Scuse me.

That's okay.

Why did **she** have to show up?

She's joined at the hip to Derek! Can't she leave him alone?

GOOFYFOOT GURL
hitting the beach this September!

THE revolve TOUR

ALL NEW EVENT for Teen Girls
PRESENTED BY WOMEN OF FAITH

We're Coming to a City Near You!
TOUR DATES

Columbus, OH
September 14 - 15, 2007

Dallas, TX
September 21 - 22, 2007

Hartford, CT
September 28 - 29, 2007

St. Louis, MO
October 5 - 6, 2007

Anaheim, CA
October 12 - 13, 2007

Sacramento, CA
October 19 - 20, 2007

Philadelphia, PA
November 2 - 3, 2007

Minneapolis, MN
November 9 - 10, 2007

Portland, OR
November 16 - 17, 2007

Atlanta, GA
November 30 - Dec. 1, 2007

Orlando, FL
January 25 - 26, 2008

Charlotte, NC
February 1 - 2, 2008

Denver, CO
February 15 - 16, 2008

Houston, TX
February 22 - 23, 2008

Hawk Nelson

Natalie Grant

KJ-52

Max & Jenna Lucado

Ayiesha Woods

Chad Eastham

Kimiko Soldati

Download **Preview Video** Online

To register by phone, call 877-9-REVOLVE
or online at REVOLVETOUR.COM

Serenity

Created by Realbuzz Studios, Inc.
Min Kwon, Primary Artist

Serenity throws a big wet sloppy one out to:
Michelle C., Noah S., Jason P., Randy M., and Jomar B.

Smack!
Luv U Guyz !!!

©&TM 2007 by Realbuzz Studios   ISBN 978-1-59554-386-8
www.Realbuzz Studios.com
www.SerenityBuzz.com

Published by Thomas Nelson, Inc. Nashville, TN 37214 www.thomasnelson.com

Library of Congress Cataloguing-in-Publication Data
Applied For

Scripture quotations marked NCV are taken from
The HOLY BIBLE, New Century VERSION®. NCV®.
Copyright © 2001 by Nelson Bibles.
Used by permission of Thomas Nelson. All rights reserved.

Printed in Singapore.
5 4 3 2 1